HERE COMES T. REX COTTONTAIL

by LOIS G. GRAMBLING • illustrated by JACK E. DAVIS

KATHERINE TEGEN BOOKS
An Imprint of HarperCollins*Publishers*

Also by Lois G. Grambling and Jack E. Davis

Here Comes T. Rex Cottontail

Text copyright © 2007 by Lois G. Grambling

Illustrations copyright © 2007 by Jack E. Davis

Manufactured in China.

www.harpercollinschildrens.com

Library of Congress Cataloging-in-Publication Data

Grambling, Lois G.

　Here comes T. Rex Cottontail / written by Lois G. Grambling ; illustrated by Jack E. Davis.— 1st ed.

　　p.　cm.

　Summary: A Tyrannosaurus rex tries his best to fill in for the sick Easter Bunny.

　ISBN-10: 0-06-053129-0 (trade bdg.) — ISBN-13: 978-0-06-053129-4 (trade bdg.)

　ISBN-10: 0-06-053131-2 (lib. bdg.) — ISBN-13: 978-0-06-053131-7 (lib. bdg.)

　[1. Easter—Fiction. 2. Tyrannosaurus rex—Fiction. 3. Dinosaurs—Fiction.] I. Davis, Jack E., ill. II. Title.

PZ7.G7655Her 2006　　　　　　　　　　　　　　　　　　　　　　　　　　　　　　2006000858

[E]—dc22　　　　　　　　　　　　　　　　　　　　　　　　　　　　　　　　　　CIP

　　　　　　　　　　　　　　　　　　　　　　　　　　　　　　　　　　　　　　AC

Typography by Jeanne L. Hogle

1 2 3 4 5 6 7 8 9 10

❖

First Edition

To my favorite Easter bunnies, some being somewhat larger
and older than others... Art, Jeff, Mark, Marcia,
Lara, Ty, Mason, and Jesse
—L.G.G.

For Jerry Stone
—J.E.D.

T. Rex was looking in the mirror.
"Not bad," he said. "Not bad at all."
Just then the doorbell rang.
He answered it.
It was his friends Diplodocus,
Stegosaurus, and Iguanodon.

"Why the funny ears? And big cotton tail?" Diplodocus asked.

"Tomorrow is Easter," Stegosaurus said, "not Halloween.

"Peter Cottontail, a.k.a. the Easter Bunny, has a cold," T. Rex said, "and he asked me to deliver his eggs tomorrow."

"But you can't hop!" Iguanodon said.

"I've been practicing," T. Rex said.

The three friends looked around.
"Where are the eggs?" they asked.
"At his house," T. Rex answered. "I'm hopping down there now to get them."
Diplodocus, Stegosaurus, and Iguanodon watched as T. Rex **WOBBLED** and **HOPPED** out the door.
"I'm afraid those eggs are in for a shell-shattering trip tomorrow," Stegosaurus said.
"T. Rex can practice when he gets back," Iguanodon said.
"Too late!" Diplodocus said, looking out the window.

Poor T. Rex!
WOBBLING and **HOPPING** up
the bumpy trail, he stumbled and
fell . . . and landed *kersplat* on
Peter Cottontail's basketful of eggs.
WHAT A MESS!

T. Rex walked slowly into
his house.
"What now?" his friends asked.
"I don't know," T. Rex answered.

Suddenly T. Rex had an idea.
"We'll get more eggs," he said, "and color them.
Then I'll have some to deliver Easter morning."

"Where will we get more eggs?" Stegosaurus asked. "Hen gave all of hers to Peter Cottontail."

"There *must* be more out there somewhere!" T. Rex said.

Diplodocus grabbed the empty basket. "You stay here and practice!" he said. "We'll get the eggs!"

By the end of the afternoon, T. Rex had
gotten the **WOBBLE** out of his **HOP**.
And his friends had gotten more eggs.
T. Rex was pleased.

"Where did you get them?" he asked.
"From Duck and
Goose and Turkey,"
Stegosaurus said.
"And one from
Screech Owl."
"We better
start coloring
them now," Iguanodon said, "or
we won't be done till dawn!"
Late that night all the
eggs were colored.
T. Rex and his friends
were asleep.
And snoring.

Unfortunately, when the sun came up, T. Rex and his friends
were still asleep.
But the children weren't. They were at their windows. Awake.
And waiting.
Shouts of

"WHERE ARE YOU, EASTER BUNNY?!" could be heard.

T. Rex heard them. He jumped up. He put on his funny ears, cotton tail, long twitching whiskers, jacket, and bow tie.

"I'll save an egg for Peter Cottontail," T. Rex said to his friends. "Meet me at his house later. We'll give it to him then," he said, hopping out the door.

The children were still at their windows.
Waiting . . . and worrying . . . until T. Rex
hopped into view!

"COOL!" they shouted.

**"THAT'S ONE REALLY BIG
COTTONTAIL HOPPING DOWN
THAT BUMPY TRAIL!"**

When all the eggs (except one) had been delivered, T. Rex started hopping back up the bumpy trail.

"Thanks for our eggs, Mister Really Big Cottontail," the children called after him.

"Anytime," T. Rex called back.

T. Rex **HOPPED** to Peter Cottontail's house.

His friends were already there. "Do you have the egg?" they asked.

T. Rex nodded and rang the doorbell.

Peter Cottontail answered it. T. Rex handed Peter Cottontail the egg.

"For me?" Peter Cottontail asked.

T. Rex and his friends nodded. "No one has ever given me an Easter egg before," he said. "Thank you."

Just then the eggs began to crack open!

CRACK   CRACK

CRACK   CRACK

And dozens of tiny ducks started *quacking*!

And dozens of tiny geese started *honking*!

And dozens of tiny turkeys started *gobbling*!

"This is the best Easter ever!" the children shouted.

Then Peter Cottontail's egg began
to crack open!

C R A C K

And one tiny screech owl started
screeching!

Peter Cottontail was surprised
and delighted.

"This is the noisiest Easter ever!"
he said. "The noisiest—and the
best! I shall never forget it."

"Nor shall we!" said T. Rex and
his friends.

QUACK!

HAPPY EASTER, EVERYBODY!